To order additional copies of this book, contact:
Xlibris
844-714-8691
www.Xlibris.com
Orders@Xlibris.com

ISBN: 978-1-6641-5167-3 (sc)
ISBN: 978-1-6641-5166-6 (e)

Print information available on the last page

Rev. date: 01/20/2021

"We love you, Dre!"

Shevonica M. Howell

Illustrated by: Farrah Prince

This book was made especially
for Andre V. Caldwell, III

Happy 3rd Birthday
2021

Dre ...

Sir/Ma'am ...

Mommy & Daddy
love you!

Andre ...

What Audre´?

I love you, little brother!

Nephew ...

Yes "TT"

I love you!

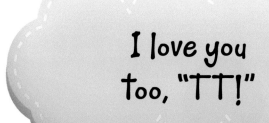

Granny's Boy...

Ma'am Granny?

I love you, grandson!

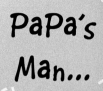

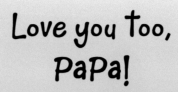

Dre, we love you!!!

SIGHT WORDS

All

Boy

Daddy

Granny

I

Love

Ma'am

Man

Mommy

PaPa

Sir

Too

We

What

You

Shevonica M. Howell is the Founder & CEO of Academy of Scholars, Inc., a private school in Jacksonville, FL. She is also the author of The "YOU TEACH IT" Math Study Guide, A Play with Words Word Search Puzzle Book, and three nonfiction books. She has a son, daughter, and two grandkids. ShevonicaMHowell@gmail.com

Farrah Milan Prince is a self-taught Artist and college student from Jacksonville, Florida. Ms. Prince is also the illustrator of What's in a Name. Ms. Prince is a passionate Artist that has always had a love for drawing and painting. Ms. Prince remains humbled and grateful to her family for believing in her craft and for blessing her with their unwavering love and support. FarrahMilan06@gmail.com

Printed in the United States
By Bookmasters